The Freedom Riddle

retold by ANGELA SHELF MEDEARIS

illustrated by JOHN WARD

LODESTAR BOOKS
Dutton   New York

in memory of Simon Brown
A. S. M.

to my forebears
J. W.

Library of Congress Cataloging-in-Publication Data

Medearis, Angela Shelf, 1956–
The Freedom riddle / adapted by Angela Shelf Medearis;
Ilustrated by John Ward.—1st ed.
p.   cm.
"Lodestar books."
Summary: Master Brown agrees to grant Jim his freedom if Jim
can stump him with a riddle.
ISBN 0-525-67469-1
(1. Folklore, Afro-American.)
I. Ward, John (John Clarence), ill. II. Title.
PZ8.1.M468Ch 1995
398.2—dc20
(E)
93-10713
CIP
AC

Published in the United States by Lodestar Books,
an affiliate of Dutton Children's Books,
a division of Penguin Books USA Inc.,
375 Hudson Street, New York, New York 10014

Published simultaneously in Canada
by McClelland & Stewart, Toronto

Editor: Rosemary Brosnan   Designer: Richard Granald

Printed in Hong Kong   First Edition
10 9 8 7 6 5 4 3 2 1

Author's Note

In 1900, when the author William J. Faulkner was a boy, an elderly man named Simon Brown was hired to work on his widowed mother's farm in South Carolina. Simon Brown told Faulkner that he had been a slave in Virginia on the same plantation as Jim, the main character of this story. He said the story was true, and that Jim had "riddled" his way to freedom.

Many of the stories that Simon Brown told young William are collected in his book *The Days When the Animals Talked,* which has been reprinted by Marie Faulkner Brown, William J. Faulkner's daughter. *The Freedom Riddle* is based on a story titled "A Riddle for Freedom." I was attracted to the story because Jim uses his brain, instead of his feet, to gain his freedom. I'd especially like to thank Mrs. Brown for her cheerful assistance and cooperation with my research.

—Angela Shelf Medearis

It was finally Christmas day! In honor of the holiday season, nature had decorated the state of Virginia with a powdery frosting of fresh snow. On this Christmas morning in 1850, a clever young man named Jim woke up with a wonderful idea. Jim was a slave and head foreman on Master Brown's plantation. For as long as Jim could remember, everyone on the plantation had played a special game on Christmas day. Whenever two people met for the first time, they quickly said "Christmas gift." Whoever said it first received a present.

Most of the time, the winner was given nutmeg-flavored cookies called tea cakes, molasses taffy, sweet-potato candy, popcorn, nuts, or a bottle of homemade syrup. But this Christmas, Jim wanted an unusual gift. He wanted to be free from slavery.

Jim had wanted his freedom ever since he was a boy. His mother, father, and brother had been sold together. The buyer wasn't interested in Jim, because he was too small to do hard work. The auctioneer had turned a deaf ear to the family's cries and had sold Jim to Master Brown. Jim never saw his family again.

Jim rolled up his quilt and dressed quickly. His footsteps made a winding path through the snow from his small cabin in the slave quarters to the Big House. As Jim passed the cookshed, he heard the cook mournfully singing a Christmas spiritual. Her lilting soprano swirled around in the frozen air, mingling with the smoke from her cookfire.

When Jim reached the Big House, he knocked on the back door. Soon, old Master Brown came out onto the porch.

"Good Morning, Master," said Jim.

"Good Morning, Jim," said Master Brown.

"Christmas gift," said Jim really fast.

"Oh, you caught me!" said Master Brown with a gruff laugh. "You said 'Christmas gift' first. So, what do you want me to give you?"

Jim looked at Master Brown for a moment. He knew Master Brown wouldn't want to give him the gift he wanted the most. Then Jim had a sudden thought. There was nothing that Master Brown loved better than a good riddle!

"I want my freedom, Master," Jim said slowly. "If I can tell you a riddle you can't solve, will you give me my freedom?"

Master Brown rubbed his chin and thought for a moment. Then he said, "Now, what would the likes of you know about riddles?"

"Well," said Jim, "I heard someone say that you'd never been stumped yet with a riddle. And I know you're a man whose word is as good as his bond."

"That's all true," said Master Brown proudly.

"I figure a smart man like you probably can guess a riddle I think up as quick as anything," said Jim. "But you might like the sport of it."

"I just might," said Master Brown. "But what do you want me to wager if I can't guess this riddle of yours?"

"I want my freedom papers," said Jim.

"If I fail to guess the answer, I'll be out a good bit of money on you," said Master Brown. "What do you stand to lose in this deal?"

"Master, you know I don't own anything," said Jim. "But I would stake my life that you can't guess my riddle."

"Seems like I'm making a bad bargain here," said Master Brown. "But there's nothing I love more than solving a good riddle. You've got yourself a wager, Jim."

Jim smiled. "I'm not quite ready with my riddle yet, Master Brown. I'll come back when I am." Jim traced his footsteps back to the quarters.

Now, Christmas was a special occasion even during those terrible days of slavery. It was one of the few times on Master Brown's plantation that the slaves could rest from their chores. Like most masters, Master Brown gave the slaves few comforts for the poor homes they lived in. Some of his slaves used this time to make new brooms, baskets, and mats for their quarters. Jim spent hours setting snares and traps in the woods for wild game. Then he joined the other young men who were running races on the plantation.

From early in the morning until noon, the air vibrated with the merry music of the colorfully dressed John Canoers. The John Canoers were a group of slaves who celebrated Christmas by performing festive songs they'd composed. Their costumes, singing, and dancing were a rollicking, rhythmic blend of African tribal customs and American holiday traditions.

The two leadmen each wore a crown of cow horns and were wrapped in a rainbow-colored net. Cow tails were fastened to their backs. The other singers and dancers were dressed in wild costumes made of dangling rags, ox and goat horns, peacock feathers, raccoon skins, and cowbells.

Some of the singers beat on a sheepskin-covered gumbo box, which was similar to a drum. Other members of the group played the fiddle, tambourines, or triangles. Those who did not have an instrument beat sticks or jawbones together, clapped their hands, and danced in time to the words of the lively songs. Usually the singers and dancers received pennies or drinks from the plantation owners for their performance. If they went to a house and did not receive any money, they would sing:

> Poor master, so they say;
> Down in the heel, so they say;
> Got no money, so they say;
> God Almighty bless you,
> so they say!

Jim wandered over to join the crowd that had gathered to celebrate with the John Canoers. He clapped along in time to the music.

One of the things Jim liked most about Christmas was all the wonderful food! He was so tired of the salt pork and cornmeal the slaves were given to eat day in and day out. On Christmas day, the good smells of roast pig, duck and goose, wild turkey, and baked chicken rose from the cookshed and filled the air. When dinner was finally served, Jim ate and ate. After dinner, he helped himself to a slice of every kind of pie. Then, Jim sampled some Scripture cake. Every ingredient in this honey-sweet cake could be found in the Bible. He also had a piece of delicious salt pork cake, which contained bits of melted salt pork. Jim wiped his mouth and settled back against the barn wall with a sigh. His stomach was full, and all around him everyone was making merry. But all Jim could think about was his freedom riddle.

The Christmas holidays came to an end, and the New Year of 1851 began. Jim still had not thought of a riddle that would stump Master Brown. The back-breaking work around the plantation began anew. The little happiness Jim had enjoyed at Christmas was soon only a memory, as the long, weary work-days stretched out before him.

The gentle spring sunshine began to melt the snow and chase away the cold. The animals began to give birth. Jim tenderly cared for a newborn filly whose mother had died during its delivery. He sor-rowfully dragged the mare's body into the woods.

Later during the spring, Jim discovered that a mother partridge had laid seven eggs in a nest she'd made inside the mare's bones. Six of the eggs in the nest had hatched. The mother nestled contentedly with her brood in the sun-bleached skeleton. Jim looked at the nest in amazement. I guess it just goes to show you that the living can make use of the dead, thought Jim.

Spring boiled into summer. The slaves worked on the plantation from sunup until sunset. As foreman, Jim had to keep an eye on the other field slaves to make sure they all did their share. Many of the slaves had worked under cruel foremen and overseers, both white and black. Jim was different. He was kind but firm.

Day after day, Jim crawled along the hot, dusty rows of cotton plants, dragging his tow sack behind him. Jim filled the bag as fast as he could. Every evening after his chores were done, Jim wearily went down the gravel path to the river to wash off the dust of the day. The sharp stones pressed into the tough soles of Jim's feet. He stooped down and brushed them off. Then he picked up a rock, tossing it gently up and down in his hand for a moment. Jim slipped the rock into his pocket and continued on his way.

When Jim reached the river, he scooped up the cool water with both hands and splashed it over his head and face. He was almost finished when he opened his eyes in surprise. The drawstring of a burlap sack was tangled around a log in the river. Jim waded out to get the sack. Inside were a pair of pants, two shirts, and a pair of knee-high boots.

Someone's clothes must have fallen overboard, thought Jim. The shirt and pants were too small. Jim stuck his feet in the boots. They fit just fine, but the toes were partially filled with mud and water. He quickly removed the boots and poured the water out. You'd think these boots were a bucket instead of something you wear on your feet, thought Jim.

The moon was up when Jim went to groom the little filly. He oiled the filly's saddle and checked the stirrups. Then he worked on a braided riding crop he was making out of strips from the dead mare's hide. As he worked, Jim thought about everything that had happened to him that day. During the long, hot summer, the parts of Jim's freedom riddle slowly began to fit together.

Harvest time came during the cooler fall days. All the field hands labored very hard to reap the crops and store them away in the barns. Every night after the chores were done, Jim lay on his quilt and worked on his riddle verse by verse. Jim had to memorize everything because he couldn't read or write. It was against the law to educate a slave in Virginia.

The cold, snowy winds of winter blew Christmas onto the plantation again. Happy cries of "Christmas

gift" were heard well before dawn around the slave quarters and at the Big House. Another long year of slavery had come and gone. But on that morning in 1851, Jim was finally ready to tell Master Brown his freedom riddle.

Riddles during that time were like jigsaw puzzles made of words. A good riddle could be pieced together in the mind when the hands were busy. Many riddle tellers spent long winter evenings stringing together tricky sets of verses peppered with special clues for their listeners. Jim made up his riddle from some of the unusual things that had happened to him over the year.

Jim nervously got ready to go up to the Big House to tell his riddle to Master Brown. He filled his old straw hat with gravel from the pathway and carefully placed it on his head. Then Jim went down to the river. He broke through the light crust of ice, took off his boots, and partially filled them with water. Jim eased his feet back into his boots. His footsteps made a squishy sound as he walked from the creek to the barn.

Jim sloshed into the barn and quickly saddled the little filly. Then he picked up the horsehide whip he had made over the summer. Jim stood up on the cold, iron stirrups and swung onto the filly's back. As he slowly rode up to the Big House, he whispered his freedom riddle over and over to himself.

Jim knocked loudly on the back door of the Big House. Master Brown opened the door and peered out. "Good morning and Merry Christmas to you, Master," said Jim.

"And to you, Jim,'' said Master Brown.

"Master, I'm ready to tell you the riddle we talked about last Christmas. The riddle for my freedom," said Jim.

"Good, Jim," said Master Brown. "I've been looking forward to this. Since today is a holiday, I believe everyone might want to be a part of the sport. It's not every day that a person hears a good riddle."

Master Brown called his family and the house servants. Then he blew the horn to call the field hands who were down in the slave quarters.

Soon everyone on the plantation was gathered on the porch and around the Big House steps. Jim noticed that his boots were slowly leaking water. "Well, now," said Jim quickly. "Last Christmas Master Brown was kind enough to wager me my freedom in exchange for a riddle he can't solve. Took me until this Christmas to put it together, but now I'm ready."

The field hands whispered excitedly among themselves.

Jim raised his hands to quiet them. "I've been here and there this year and I've seen many interesting things." Jim felt a piece of gravel slip out from underneath his hat and trickle down his back. He rushed on. "I delivered this filly here, when its mama died. I got rid of the body but the bones remain. I saved strips of the mare's hide." Jim gently tapped the filly with his horsehide whip. "I've seen a partridge lay seven eggs in a mighty odd place, and somewhere those six chicks are flying free." Jim took a deep breath. "I've ridden in these stirrups with my head under a rocky burden and with my feet in the river. So, there are your clues. Now, ya'll know that there is nothing more puzzling than daily living, so that's what my riddle's about." Then Jim slowly told them his freedom riddle.

Old eighteen hundred and fifty-one,
Out of the dead the living came.
Seven there were, but six there be.
Under the gravel, I do travel,
On the cold iron, I do stand.
I ride the filly never foaled
and hold the damsel in my hand.
Water knee-deep on the man,
and not a drop do you see.
I'm innocent, now set me free.

Master Brown listened carefully to Jim's riddle. He rubbed his chin and thought and thought about each clue Jim had given. He walked back and forth, back and forth, down the wide porch. Then he gave

the best answer he could to one verse and then another. Jim slowly shook his head, wrong and wrong again.

Drip, drip, drip. The water trickling from Jim's boots splashed on the filly and made her skittish. Master Brown continued to pace. Sweat slid down Jim's face and settled in his shirt collar. The crowd shifted restlessly in the cool morning air. Back and forth, back and forth, paced Master Brown. But try as he might, he couldn't think of the answer to Jim's riddle. His face turned red, and he clenched his fists. Jim was his very best plow hand, and he didn't want to lose him.

At last Master Brown said to Jim with a sigh, "All right, Jim, I give up. You've won your freedom. Now what's the answer to this riddle of yours?"

Jim clapped his hands and smiled happily. Shouts of joy rang out among the house servants and the field hands. "Thank you, Master Brown," Jim said. "Now here's the answer to my riddle."

Old eighteen hundred and fifty-one,

"Now that part is easy," said Jim. "It happened this year."

Out of the dead the living came.

"One day while I was walking in the woods, I saw a partridge and six of her newly hatched chicks inside a mare's skeleton," said Jim.

Seven there were, but six there be.

"You remember that I told you the partridge laid seven eggs, and six chicks were flying free? That's because only six of the eggs hatched," said Jim.

Under the gravel, I do travel,

Jim removed his hat and poured the gravel onto the ground. "This was the rocky burden I've been traveling under."

On the cold iron, I do stand.

Jim stood up in the iron stirrups of the saddle.

I ride the filly never foaled
and hold the damsel in my hand.

"This filly's mama died before she finished giving birth," said Jim. "So the filly was never foaled." Then he held up his horsehide whip. "This whip I'm holding is made out of the mare's hide."

Water knee-deep on the man,
and not a drop do you see.

Jim smiled and poured out the water that filled his knee-high boots. "I got this water from the river," Jim said.

I'm innocent, now set me free.

I'm surely an innocent man, Master Brown," said Jim. "And now I'm a free man too! Merry Christmas, everyone!" Jim threw his hat into the air and rode off across the fields on the little filly. And from that day on, Jim was never a slave anymore.